A KITTEN IN
GOOSEBERRY PA

A KITTEN IN
GOOSEBERRY PARK

CYNTHIA RYLANT ❦ ARTHUR HOWARD

Beach Lane Books New York London Toronto Sydney New Delhi

BEACH LANE BOOKS
An imprint of Simon & Schuster Children's Publishing Division
1230 Avenue of the Americas, New York, New York 10020
This book is a work of fiction. Any references to historical events, real people, or real places are used fictitiously. Other names, characters, places, and events are products of the author's imagination, and any resemblance to actual events or places or persons, living or dead, is entirely coincidental.
Text © 2022 by Cynthia Rylant
Illustration © 2022 by Arthur Howard
Jacket design by Irene Metaxatos © 2022 by Simon & Schuster, Inc.
For information about special discounts for bulk purchases, please contact Simon & Schuster Special Sales at 1-866-506-1949 or business@simonandschuster.com.
The Simon & Schuster Speakers Bureau can bring authors to your live event. For more information or to book an event, contact the Simon & Schuster Speakers Bureau at 1-866-248-3049 or visit our website at www.simonspeakers.com.
Interior design by Irene Metaxatos
The text for this book was set in Guardi LT Std.
The illustrations for this book were rendered in pencil, India ink, and wash.
Manufactured in the United States of America
0222 FFG
First Edition
2 4 6 8 10 9 7 5 3 1
Library of Congress Cataloging-in-Publication Data
Names: Rylant, Cynthia, author. | Howard, Arthur, illustrator.
Title: A kitten in Gooseberry Park / Cynthia Rylant ; illustrated by Arthur Howard.
Description: First edition. | New York : Beach Lane Books, [2022] | Series: Gooseberry Park | Audience: Ages 8-12. | Audience: Grades 4-6. | Summary: Kona the labrador, Gwendolyn the hermit crab, and Murray the bat help a lost bobcat kitten find his family after being swept down the mountain from the rain.
Identifiers: LCCN 2021013321 (print) | LCCN 2021013322 (ebook) | ISBN 9781534494503 (hardcover) | ISBN 9781534494527 (ebook)
Subjects: CYAC: Lost children—Fiction. | Bobcat—Fiction. | Animals—Infancy—Fiction. | Animals—Fiction.
Classification: LCC PZ7.R982 Km 2022 (print) | LCC PZ7.R982 (ebook) | DDC [Fic]—dc23
LC record available at https://lccn.loc.gov/2021013321
LC ebook record available at https://lccn.loc.gov/2021013322

Contents

1

Deluge

Remember when we wished for rain?" Kona asked his best friend, Gwendolyn. The Labrador turned his large brown head away from the picture window and looked toward the clear bowl on Professor Albert's coffee table.

"Indeed we did," answered the hermit crab, her antennae bending toward the wet deluge outside.

It had been over a year

since they'd lived through the drought, those many months of no rain at all that had brought hard times to Kona's and Gwendolyn's friends who lived nearby in Gooseberry Park. Over a year since the two had done their part to deliver water to the babies and elders of the park when the dry situation became desperate.

The drought had been long. It had been fearful. But it had broken, finally, with the long-awaited arrival of rain, and everyone in Gooseberry Park had survived. Nature had settled back into its ordinary ways: a bit of sun here, some rain there, now and then snow. There was the occasional surprise storm that kept everyone inside. But nature, for more than a year now, had been ordinary.

Until lately. Lately, nature had not been ordinary. The rain did not seem to know when to stop. Outside Professor Albert's picture window pounded a heavy, loud drumming-drumming of water. Rain had been falling for days.

Both Kona and Gwendolyn loved rain. They

loved being wet. When Professor Albert reached for his raincoat and umbrella, Kona always did a little dance at the door, for he knew they were going to the park. Rain never stopped Professor Albert. And because he was a very careful

pet owner, he put a bright red doggy raincoat on Kona as well. The slick coat wrapped around the Labrador and closed snugly under the dog's middle. Labradors love water—they are famous for plunging with all fours into lakes all over the world. Kona did not really need a coat. But it did keep him mostly dry and tidy, which made things

4

easier on the return home. Neither Professor Albert nor Kona wished to have a wet and sloppy house.

And Gwendolyn: Well, she loved water very much because near water is the natural home of hermit crabs. Professor Albert had remembered this and had furnished her bowl with a small pool of water and a plastic palm tree. He wanted both of his pets to be happy. And they were.

Of course, Professor Albert would have been greatly surprised if someone had told him that he also had a third pet. Of sorts. A sort-of pet who pilfered his cheese puffs and borrowed his television to watch *Jeopardy!* This sort-of pet had his own home in a tree in Gooseberry Park, but because he was a sociable bat—yes, a bat—he spent a lot of his free time with his friends Kona and Gwendolyn on Miller Street. He had met Kona by way of Stumpy Squirrel, and now he visited frequently, telling Kona and Gwendolyn all the park news between snacks from the kitchen. Professor Albert had no idea, though he did sometimes wonder where the pretzels went.

Kona and Gwendolyn gazed together at the heavy streams of water rushing down the street, at the birdbaths overflowing, at the rain gutters gushing small waterfalls onto Professor Albert's boxwoods below. They did not know that the professor's sort-of pet—a bat named Murray— would soon make a bold and drippy flight to see them. And to tell them what he had found.

2
Bat Feet

Tap-tap-tap.
Tappity-tap.

There are not many Labrador retrievers who recognize the sound of little bat feet upon anodized aluminum, but Kona—stretched out on his dog bed and, until now, dreaming of garlic biscuits—knew the sound of a persistent bat when he heard one.

"Gwendolyn, are you awake?" asked Kona. "Murray's outside."

"I know, dear," said the hermit crab, waving a claw at the wet creature now doing a tap dance on the windowsill. "What is he doing here at this hour?"

"I hope it's not because he needs an Oreo," said Kona, checking the clock. Two in the morning!

"Surely not," said Gwendolyn as Kona gently lifted her from the bowl so she could unlock the front door. "Even Murray wouldn't travel in this rain at this hour for a cookie."

"Eee *ite*," said Kona as he held her shell in his teeth.

"Well, yes," she agreed intuitively. "He might."

When they opened the door,

8

Murray hopped inside and began shaking himself dry on Kona's rug beside the fireplace.

"Monsoon! Typhoon!" cried Murray. "Living room!"

Shake, shake, shake, flap, flap.

"Murray, it's two o'clock in the morning," said Kona. "And pouring."

"Rain waits for no bat!" said Murray.

Shake. Flap. Shake.

Murray suddenly stopped shaking and flapping and looked toward Professor Albert's kitchen cabinets.

"Tell us you didn't wake us up for an Oreo," said Kona.

Murray looked at his two friends and gasped. "Never!" said the bat. "But hold that thought!"

Murray spread his wings wide, the fire behind him giving them a dramatic neon glow.

"You will never guess what I found," he announced.

"Oh dear," said Gwendolyn. "Is it something having to do with chopsticks and duck sauce?"

"Certainly not!" said the offended little bat. "Although, actually, yes, in a way. Good guess!"

Kona groaned. "It *is* about food," he said. "At two o'clock in the morning."

"It is about me risking wet life and wet limb to fly all the way from Norm's Chinese Diner to Miller Street because we have a *crisis*!" said Murray. "A cute crisis, I must say, but still a *crisis*!"

"Whatever are you talking about, dear?" asked

Gwendolyn. "Are you sure you don't need to breathe?"

"No thanks," said Murray. "These bat lungs are doing great. And it's a good thing, because I flew all the way from Norm's Chinese."

"For *what*?" asked Kona. "What?"

"A kitten," said Murray with a grin.

"A what?" asked Kona and Gwendolyn together.

"A kitten," said Murray. "And it's a *big* one!"

3

A Crisis!

Gooseberry Park was beautiful every season of the year. In spring there were forsythias and azaleas along the walking paths. In summer irises bloomed beside the water gardens full of floating lily pads. In winter the holly bushes made bright crimson berries.

But fall seemed to be everyone's favorite season in Gooseberry Park. Life became a dazzling painting. Bright yellow and orange and red leaves fluttered on the tall trees, then finally drifted to

the ground, casting that sweet leafy scent that signals harvest: the harvest of brown nuts, of hard apples, of blackberries still lingering on the bush.

For many of the park's residents, fall necessarily

had to be a time of storing up, since winter would be the *next* season. Unlike the snakes and the lizards, who would be sleeping all winter, most of the park animals would be up and about all the way to spring, and they needed to be thinking about supper. And lunch. And breakfast. For January! Well-stocked pantries and root cellars: These were the talk of the park in fall.

As a result, most creatures were busy hunting and gathering. Even as the rain fell.

And this turned out to be very lucky for a certain kitten. A certain kitten who had been hiding under the dumpster of Norm's Chinese Diner the very night a certain bat had gone foraging for some fortune cookies.

"I was looking for fortune cookies," Murray told Kona and Gwendolyn as he stretched out his toes to dry. "For Stumpy's pantry. Oh, my toesies feel toasty!"

Stumpy Squirrel was Murray's tree mate in Gooseberry Park. Murray lived upstairs and

Stumpy lived down, with her three children, Top, Bottom, and Sparrow. Kona and Gwendolyn had an adventurous history with Stumpy Squirrel, including the Christmas they babysat her children during an ice storm. Friendships forged in ice storms always last.

"Can you believe some people throw away fortune cookies without even opening the wrapper and reading the fortune?" asked Murray. "I can't count the number of times I've been promised a long, happy life and a mug."

Murray grinned.

"Just kidding about the mug," he said.

"We know, dear," said Gwendolyn.

"The *kitten*," said Kona impatiently.

"Well, as you know," said Murray, "it's been raining."

Kona and Gwendolyn nodded. Murray turned around to warm his tummy.

"And did you also know that there are big ditches up on the mountain called gullies?" said Murray.

"How do you know about gullies?" asked Kona.

"The kitten told me," said Murray.

"How could a kitten know about gullies up on the mountain?" asked Kona.

16

"So many questions!" said Murray. "You're interrupting my dramatic arc!"

He paused for effect.

"The kitten . . . ," said Murray with a slow-building pace, "knows about gullies up on the mountain . . . because . . ."

"Yes?" said Kona.

"He's a *BOBCAT*!" Murray shrieked.

"BOBCAT?" Kona and Gwendolyn both repeated. Kona added a "Shhh." Professor Albert

slept like a boulder, but it was always prudent to keep their voices down.

"Can you believe it?" asked Murray.

"Hardly," answered Kona.

"Are you certain?" asked Gwendolyn. "Perhaps he is just a well-fed tabby."

"Oh, I'm sure he's a bob- cat," said Murray. "He has those black tufties on top of his ears. And besides, he told me. He told me all about taking a walk with his mama, and his mama told him to be very careful of the gullies. Because the gullies weren't just big ditches anymore. They were practically raging rivers because of all the rain! And Kitten *tried* to be careful—oh, I'm about to get teary—but he slipped and went right in one!"

"My," said Gwendolyn.

"Awful," said Kona.

"And he was swept away from his mama!" said

Murray, his bat wings wide and his bat eyes big for more drama. "Does anyone have a hankie?"

"No," said Kona.

"Try to go on, dear," said Gwendolyn.

"Well," said Murray, "the kitten washed down the mountain into a drain that went right by Norm's. So he climbed out of the drain and hid under the dumpster. It always smells like egg rolls, so who wouldn't?"

Kona and Gwendolyn were silent while Murray waited for more gasps and *amazing*s.

Finally Kona said, "Murray, are you making all this up because you just really need an Oreo?"

"It's all true, cross my little bat heart," said Murray, his wing marking an

X on his chest. "We have a bobcat in the family now."

"I do love children," said Gwendolyn.

"We know," said Murray. "You have children everywhere!"

"Near practically every major body of water," said Gwendolyn. "Babies are quite wonderful."

"We can't raise a bobcat!" said Kona.

"Oh no, dear," answered Gwendolyn. "I was just remembering babies in general. And besides," she added, "somewhere up on that mountain is a mama quite beside herself."

"Is the kitten still at Norm's?" Kona asked Murray.

"Yes," said Murray. "I gave him six egg rolls and told him not to move—or meow—until I get back."

"We have a crisis," said Kona.

20

A Crisis!

"I already told you that!" said Murray.

"Maybe there's a hollow log in the park we can keep him in until we find his mother," said Kona.

"Okay, but it's going to take more than six egg rolls a day to keep that baby fed," said Murray. "I repeat: The kitten is *big*."

Murray looked toward Professor Albert's kitchen cabinets again.

"Oh no," said Kona. "We can't. Not that food. The professor will think his memory problems have come back. Remember when you stole his food for Stumpy's babies? And it wasn't memory problems. It was a *bat*!"

"A bat with a heart," said Murray.

"We know, dear," said Gwendolyn.

"Plus a taste for corn chips," added Murray. "Kitten would love those."

"Kitten will eat dog food," said Kona. "The professor buys the twenty-five-pound bags— he'll never miss it. He'll just think I have a hearty appetite."

"Drat," said Murray. "No cheese-and-olive trays?"

Kona shook his head.

"Someone needs to move that kitten soon," said Gwendolyn. "And prepare a cozy log. Poor, frightened baby."

"Don't worry," said Murray. "I'll stop and tell Stumpy on my way to fetch the kitten. Stumpy

knows how to make a cozy home better than anybody."

"That she does," said Gwendolyn. "She's a good mother. She will know just how to make him feel safe and warm."

"We need to think about finding that mama bobcat, Gwendolyn," said Kona.

"Yes," said Murray. "You two solve all the problems, and I'll provide the entertainment."

"I am already thinking," said Gwendolyn, waving her antennae.

Kona and Murray filled a plastic baggie with dog kibble for the kitten.

"Try to keep the food dry," said Kona.

"Zip it up, and I'll be very gentle with my toesies," Murray answered.

They looked at the hard rain falling outside.

"Be careful flying," said Kona.

"Don't worry," the bat said with a grin. "I'm waterproof!"

"You deserve a cookie," said Kona.

"I sure do!" said Murray.

Kona and Gwendolyn watched as the little bat flew off with an Oreo in his mouth and a baggie of dog kibble in his toes, his wings beating madly against the force of the rain. Then they looked at each other. It was time to start thinking.

4

Scanning

Long friendship is such a comfort. It seemed to Kona and Gwendolyn that they had been friends all their lives, even though Gwendolyn had already lived a long life before they met. They both knew it was a wonder they had even met at all.

Professor Albert had always lived alone, but when he retired, this began to wear. He started feeling lonely because he had no one else in his house to talk to. A person does sometimes want to say something that is actually listened to by someone else, even if it is only, "I think the hedge needs pruning."

Professor Albert decided he needed a pet. But he wanted to ease into pet ownership. He wanted a pet that was not much trouble. So he went to a pet store in town, and he chose a hermit crab.

But not-much-trouble was not the real reason Professor Albert chose Gwendolyn to be his pet. He chose Gwendolyn because the moment he saw her, he thought she was beautiful and special. He was right about both, of course. Gwendolyn was an old soul, and the soul always grows more beautiful and special with age. When a hermit crab—or anyone—has lived beyond one hundred years, the soul shines like the sun.

The professor carried his hermit crab home in a little box and named her after his mother (an honor for a hermit crab who had been a mother many times over). Professor Albert finally had a house-mate to talk to, and both were happy and content.

Time passed, and then one day it dawned on Professor Albert that he needed to be more out and about in nature: He needed more trees, more birds, more blue sky and fresh air. He needed walks in Gooseberry Park.

He was not naturally a walking-about type of person. He liked books and microscopes and educational television. He liked naps. In fact, he knew that he was probably taking more naps than were good for him.

So the professor decided to get a second pet. He had become a confident pet owner, thanks to Gwendolyn. He would get a second pet, one that needed walking.

He heard about a nice woman over on Paradise Lane who had an entire large litter of Labrador puppies. One thing led to another, and one afternoon the professor found himself at a house on Paradise Lane surrounded by all of them. He watched them rolling, running, licking, and bouncing and wondered how he would ever choose one to take home. But the problem was solved entirely for him when a little chocolate Labrador puppy crawled up into the professor's lap and chose *him*.

It was Kona, of course. Or would be when Professor Albert took him home and named him after a favorite coffee.

Gwendolyn was delighted. She loved watching Kona romp and play and chew and snore
and gobble up kibble. She loved watching him
grow.

And she helped him grow too, in her way.
At night Gwendolyn told the young Labrador
all about the meaning of life, what was most

important, how to be brave, how to be good. Kona listened very carefully.

And now here they were, this rainy night, these two who had been friends for what seemed forever, with a new and unexpected but important and meaningful problem: a child lost from his mama.

"Do you know anything about bobcats, Gwendolyn?" Kona asked.

"I believe they are quite strong climbers," said Gwendolyn.

"That's good," said Kona.

The two were silent for several minutes.

"Have you come up with a plan yet?" Kona finally asked. He had great confidence in Gwendolyn to come up with a plan.

"No, dear," said Gwendolyn. "But I am scanning."

The Labrador nodded and was quiet again. He knew that "scanning" meant that Gwendolyn was searching the memory books of her long life. He watched the rain and waited.

"Transportation," Gwendolyn said suddenly.

"Transportation?" repeated Kona.

"We cannot expect the mama bobcat to come to town search-  ing for her kitten," said Gwendolyn. "She surely thinks he is still somewhere up on the mountain."

"Right," said Kona.

"So we have to put the kitten back up there," said Gwendolyn, waving her antennae upward for emphasis.

"Up on the mountain . . . impossible . . . ," began Kona.

"Not with the right transportation and the help of a sneaky little bat," answered Gwendolyn.

"Murray?" asked Kona. "What does Murray know about transportation?"

"Nothing, dear, I'm sure. But Murray knows all

about hiding. And derring-do," said Gwendolyn. "Let us find a highway map in the professor's Mini Cooper and take a look at that mountain. Then we can hatch a plan."

Kona was not sure he would be much of a hatcher.

But he quickly finished up his last garlic biscuit—Kona was always hungrier when the nearly impossible was about to happen—then picked up his good friend for the beginning of what would probably be another extraordinary adventure together.

5

Gooseberry Park

The next afternoon Kona walked to Gooseberry Park with Professor Albert, both in raincoats, the professor also in galoshes. Kona managed to steer their walk toward the sugar maple tree where Murray and Stumpy and the children lived. Kona had learned through experience that if he stopped beneath the sugar maple and started barking, the professor would allow him to run loose around the base of the tree for a while. The professor thought that Kona needed to bark up a tree because he was a dog. He did not know that Kona was just pretending to bark up a tree so that he could have a conversation with one of the tree's residents.

Today it was Stumpy who poked her head through one of the holes in the sugar maple.

"Kona!" she called. "We have Kitten!"

"Good!" said Kona. "How is he?"

The professor was examining mushrooms nearby on the ground and paid no attention to the redheaded squirrel chatting with his dog.

"Excellent health," said Stumpy. "One new tooth coming in. A bit stinky—we need to think about a bath."

"Of course," said Kona.

"And *curious*! Oh my goodness," said Stumpy, "I'd forgotten how curious babies can be."

"They can," said Kona, remembering the time

when he was a puppy and became curious about what Professor Albert's books on the nightstand would taste like. He chewed through one biography, three science fictions, and a refrigerator repair manual. After that, Professor Albert kept his books in a box until Kona was grown.

"And as a result of Kitten's curiosity," continued Stumpy, "I'm afraid Morton is going to have a bit of a surprise when he gets back home."

Morton was Murray's older brother who lived in a birch tree near Stumpy and Murray's sugar maple. Morton liked to improve himself and was now away on a silent retreat. But he had been sending Murray blank postcards to let everyone know he was fine.

"Oh my," said Kona, "what has Kitten done?"

"Well," said Stumpy, "Murray wanted to show Kitten our houses. It would be a bit of a squeeze—seems Kitten is growing by the hour—but Murray wanted him to feel at home with us all."

"Right," said Kona.

"So Kitten," Stumpy continued, "squeezed into our house first. And I showed him my shiny chain collection and my sugar packet collection and, of course, my bouncy ball collection."

"Of course," said Kona.

"Kitten then squeezed into Murray's house," continued Stumpy, "but there were so many empty take-out boxes that Kitten had to squeeze right out again."

"You know how Murray hates to cook," said Kona.

"Yes," said Stumpy.
"So Murray decided he would show Morton's house to Kitten instead."

"Oh no," said Kona.

"Exactly," said Stumpy. "Morton's perfectly arranged, one-with-the-universe Zen sanctuary in a tree."

"Don't tell me," said Kona.

"Well," said Stumpy, "since Kitten is curious and also just a baby and also unfamiliar with the word 'retract' . . ."

"Retract?" repeated Kona.

38

"Yes," continued Stumpy. "When Kitten got curious and jumped onto the waterbed to see what a floaty bed feels like, Murray told him to *retract* his claws."

"Most people would just say 'Pull in your claws!'" said Kona. "Murray watches too many science shows on PBS."

"Yes. Well, Kitten did not *retract* his claws," said Stumpy. She took a deep breath.

"And," she continued, "Murray says you'd never guess how much water a waterbed holds until it starts pouring all over the floor."

Kona groaned.

"And the meditation mat and the gong," added Stumpy.

"Morton has a gong?" asked Kona.

Stumpy nodded. "A wet one," she said.

Kona groaned again.

"But don't worry," said Stumpy. "We all told Kitten that we knew he didn't mean to claw the waterbed, and Sparrow dried off his paws, and Top and Bottom sopped up the water with my napkin collection."

"You had to donate your napkin collection?" asked Kona.

"I'll start another one," said Stumpy.

"So what did Murray do to help?" asked Kona.

"He brought us a box of Girl Scout cookies," said Stumpy.

"That was nice," said Kona.

"Kitten is a good baby," Stumpy said. "We already love him. Bottom even let Kitten play with his badminton birdie, and Bottom never shares that treasure with anyone."

"That's good to hear," answered Kona.

"Kitten is tucked into a hollow log now, napping," said Stumpy, pointing. "I fixed him a cozy bed with my wool mitten collection."

"It's good there was a hollow log so close by," said Kona.

"Yes," agreed Stumpy. "The raccoon living there just missed her mother too much and moved back home last week."

"Has Kitten eaten something?" asked Kona.

"A big helping of kibble and half of Murray's fried wontons," answered Stumpy.

Kona noticed Professor Albert picking up some soggy mushrooms with his handkerchief and putting them in his pocket to study later. It was time to go.

"I'll be back tonight," Kona told Stumpy as he turned to catch up to the professor. "We can all put our heads together then."

He barked some barks at the tree so the professor would be satisfied that they had each enjoyed a small adventure.

"See you then!" Stumpy called. She waved good-bye as Kona and the professor squished and slogged homeward.

"What a time for Herman to be out of town," Kona said to Gwendolyn when he arrived home. He lay down by the fire to dry off while Professor Albert heated up some tomato soup.

Herman was a mathematical crow who lived in Gooseberry Park, and he was a great problem solver. But Herman was in the suburbs now, spending time with his cousins on his mother's side.

"I do think we are going to need an extra

someone to help Kitten get back home," Kona continued. "Someone who really knows the mountain."

"I have been thinking that exactly," answered Gwendolyn. "Someone with wings and a good eye."

Kona could smell the tomato soup in the kitchen. It was time to sit beside the kitchen table and wait for a slice of soupy bread.

"I think what we need," said Gwendolyn, "is a Canada goose. The geese will be all over the park now, congregating and getting ready to fly south. I'm sure we can find one of them to help."

"Why a goose?" asked Kona, already wondering if they bit dogs' noses.

"Because they migrate, dear," explained Gwendolyn. "Canada geese know everything there is to know about the lay of the land. And they do look so magnificent in their V formation, don't you think? I believe a goose could find that bobcat mama."

Kona let out a deep sigh. "It is exhausting to

strike up conversations with total strangers," he said. "Especially the ones with big beaks."

"Canada geese are very approachable, dear," said Gwendolyn. "Try not to worry."

"I think I need some soup," said Kona. "And a nap."

"Yes," said Gwendolyn. "Soup and naps always prepare one for great things."

"I hope so," answered Kona. "I'll save a piece of bread for you."

"That would be divine," Gwendolyn said.

6

An Important
Meeting

Later in the evening, after Professor Albert had gone to bed, Gwendolyn unlocked the door, and Kona was on his way to Gooseberry Park again. Kona had not gotten much sleep lately, it seemed his feet were always wet, a road map was spinning in his head, and now he was carrying a baggie of kibble to a bobcat.

What had happened to normal life?

Kona did, though, so love being out in the

deep of night. And, blessedly, the days of rain had finally ended. Kona was a good dog and never sneaked out of the house unless there was an emergency. But when Kona did have to journey alone under a dark sky, everything in shadow, the clouds lit by the moon, stillness, suspense . . . he was softly thrilled.

Everyone was there, in a picnic shelter near the sugar maple, when Kona arrived. Kitten and his new friends Top, Bottom, and Sparrow were listening to Murray describe the various varieties of doughnuts.

"Jelly ones you can squirt!" Murray was saying as Kona approached.

"Hello, Kitten," said Kona, wagging his tail in a friendly way. Kitten did not run when he saw the dog, for everyone had told him about the chocolate Labrador who would help him go home.

"Hello," said Kitten shyly, lowering his eyes.

"Hi, Kona!" said the children.

"Kona!" said Murray. "You're here. Just in time to hear about tasty bear claws!"

"What?" squeaked Kitten.

"Not real bear claws, kiddo," said Murray. "These doughnuts only look like bear claws. Nobody wants to get between a bear and his claws!"

"Mama knows a bear," said Kitten.

"I'd love to meet a bear," said Sparrow.

"Me too," said Top and Bottom together.

"Doughnuts!" said Murray. "Have we forgotten that the subject was doughnuts?"

"What's a doughnut?" asked Kitten.

Murray looked at Kona. "I'm going to have to

take this kid to Hole-in-One for breakfast," he said.

"Actually, you're going to have to take Kitten a lot farther than that," Kona said.

It was time for a new subject. The subject would be *transportation*.

Stumpy put aside the fern collection she'd been sorting and prepared to listen. This was an important meeting. This was about saving Kitten.

Kona carefully explained the transportation plan he and Gwendolyn had designed. He was frequently interrupted:

"What?!"

"A *what*?!"

"In a *what*?!"

"*Then* what?!"

But Murray zeroed right in on the most important, the most *essential* element of the transportation plan:

"I am pretty sure truck stops have thousands of doughnuts," said Murray.

He looked at Kona.

"It's brilliant!" Murray shouted. "I'm in!"

Kona and Gwendolyn's idea to hide Kitten inside a truck that would travel up the mountain was approved by all. But there was still the question of where to find a truck stop where they would find a truck. And also the questions of how to get Kitten out of the truck once he got in and where on the mountain that would happen.

"Well, Kitten remembered something important," said Stumpy, looking over at Kitten, who nodded his head proudly.

"You did?" Kona asked Kitten.

"Something he saw up on the mountain

with his mama," said Stumpy.

"What did you see, Kitten?" asked Kona.

Kitten concentrated for the right words.

"Place for trucks," he answered.

"And barking," added Stumpy. "Kitten heard a lot of barking."

"Kitten!" said Kona. "That is so helpful!"

"Then I go splash," said Kitten.

"Oh dear," said Sparrow. She had become very protective of Kitten. She gave him a hug.

"Gwendolyn says that the Canada geese know the mountain very well," said Kona. "Maybe one of them will know the place that Kitten is describing."

"*Yes!*" said all three children, clapping.

"And maybe the goose can find Kitten's

mama," said Top. "She must be so worried."

Kitten suddenly looked very sad.

"Kitten hungry," he said. He sometimes got "sad" and "hungry" mixed up when explaining his feelings.

"Come on, dear," said Sparrow. "I'll fix you a nice supper of kibble and chestnuts on the picnic table over there."

"Mmmm," said Kitten, padding after her.

"So now our next step is finding a goose," said Kona. "Stumpy, can you introduce me? I'm a bit concerned for my nose."

"Certainly," said Stumpy. "But it's a friendly bunch here in the park. All Canadians, beautiful manners. Nothing like those wild ganders over on Silver Lake."

Kona was just about to go into the finer details of the transportation plan with Murray and Stumpy when out of the darkness emerged an old acquaintance.

"Hey," said the cat. It was Conroy, a local

house cat who liked to prowl.

"I heard there was a kitten," he said. "Thought I'd stop by."

"It's a bobcat," said Bottom.

"Sure, right, kid," said Conroy with a grin.

"Seriously," said Top.

"Hey, if it's a kitten, it's a kitten," said Conroy. "Where is he?"

"Over there," said both Top and Bottom, pointing to the table on the other side of the picnic shelter.

Conroy took a good long look at Kitten, who had just finished his supper.

"That appears to be a bobcat," said Conroy.

"Told you," answered both Top and Bottom.

"Cool," said Conroy. He flicked his tail a couple

of times, then strolled over to chat with Kitten. Everyone watched and waited.

Kitten was so happy to see another cat! He jumped and danced all around Conroy, rubbed up against the tabby's body, rolled over, threw all four paws in the air, and waited to play.

Conroy, however, was much too cool to play. He did want to help out the kid, though. Cat to cat.

Conroy decided to encourage Kitten to clean up. So Conroy began taking a bath. First he washed his paws. When Kitten saw this, he sat up and began washing his paws. Then Conroy washed his face. Kitten washed his face.

"Amazing," said Kona as the mutual cleanup continued.

"Well, Kitten was pretty muddy," said Stumpy.

"I don't know why they don't just use the birdbaths like I do," said Murray. "It's a lot more refreshing!"

As Conroy and Kitten were finishing up their baths, another park visitor stepped out of the darkness.

It was a weasel.

"What?" Murray shouted. "You can't weasel your way in here!"

Murray was no fan of weasels. They all lived on the west side, and everybody on that side of the park complained about weasels always talking them out of their stuff. Murray and Stumpy—stuff lovers for sure—never trusted anything a weasel said.

"I hear there's some kind of wildcat here," the weasel said in a low voice.

"Bob," said Murray.

"Don't know a Bob," said the weasel. "Name's Felix."

"Bobcat!" shouted Murray. Weasels were obviously stupid, too.

"Bobcat?" said the weasel. "Let me see him."

Kona stepped in front of the weasel. But the crafty creature just ducked under him.

"Oh, there he is," said Felix.

Sparrow was taking Kitten for one of their little walks. She used a pair of string mittens. Sparrow carried one mitten and Kitten carried the other, and the string in between kept them together.

Felix walked over to them.

"Wow, look at the size of that cat," the weasel said to no one in particular.

Sparrow frowned and pulled the mitten string

to bring Kitten closer. Kona also drew nearer. And Conroy's fur was standing straight up while his tail twitched madly. No one trusted Felix.

"Relax, everybody," said the weasel. "Just looking, is all."

But no one believes a weasel who says he is just looking. Weasels are conniving. Always ready to take advantage. *What's in it for me?* is the weasel motto.

The air was tense. The group was silent. Kitten tried to pay attention, but he was getting sleepy. Just as he opened his mouth to yawn . . .

"Bombs away!" shouted Murray, suddenly diving down from a tree.

Two jumbo marbles landed right on the weasel's head. *Crack! Crack!*

"Ouch! Ouch!" yelled Felix.

"Heading back to reload my toesies!" shouted Murray.

58

"No!" said Felix. "I'm leaving!"

He rubbed the two fresh lumps on top of his head.

"Just wanted to see the cat," he muttered. "He's not much to look at anyway."

"MEOWWWWW!" yelled Conroy. He had had enough of the weasel's weaselly ways, and he took off chasing that weasel all the way back to the west side.

Sparrow hugged Kitten.

"See, even Conroy loves you," she said.

"Kitten hungry," said Kitten, who had not understood a word the weasel had said and thought he and Conroy had run off to play.

"Do you mean 'sleepy'?" asked Sparrow.

"Sleepy," said Kitten.

"Okey-doke, then," said Sparrow. She led Kitten back to his warm log.

Murray landed with a bounce beside Kona.

"It was Top's idea to use the jumbo marbles," the bat said, grinning.

Top ran up, nodding proudly.

"Great work," said Kona.

"And Conroy!" said Murray. "I didn't know that cat had it in him!"

"Well, now we need to start thinking about what Kitten saw and heard on top of the mountain," said Kona. "I'm sure Gwendolyn will know what to do with that new information."

"Okay!" said Murray.

"And Stumpy and I will find a goose tomorrow," said Kona.

"Right!" said Murray. "Almost time to roll!"

Everyone knew that wheels were the only way they would get that baby home.

7

Forty-Eight of Them

AHNK-AHNK-AHNK-AHNK-AHNK-AHNK-AHNK-AHNK-AHNK-AHNK-AHNK-AHNK.

The next day Kona stood with Stumpy under a tree in Gooseberry Park and watched as a huge flock of Canada geese circled overhead, preparing for a landing near the lily ponds. Professor

Albert was busy elsewhere collecting cattails for his fall flower arrangements.

"How will you know which one to talk to when they land?" asked Kona.

"Don't worry," said Stumpy. "I'll hop among them and ask some questions. Geese are used to squirrels—we're everywhere."

"There are so many of them. And awfully loud," said Kona.

"Yes," said Stumpy. "Those long necks produce quite a honk."

Suddenly, with a great deal of noise and flapping, the flock swooped downward, landing belly-first in the pond or feetfirst on the grass. Then they began gobbling up the juicy green shoots all around them. Migrating requires energy, which requires food. Honks were replaced by the quiet of munching and crunching.

"I'll go over now," said Stumpy, and she ran in their direction.

Stumpy mixed about with the large flock on

the grass, hopping among them and pretending to look for buried nuts. *She looks so small,* thought Kona.

He watched as Stumpy stopped and had a word with one goose after another. Some geese couldn't talk because their mouths were full, but others seemed very chatty, their heads nodding energetically as Stumpy spoke to them.

Soon three geese and Stumpy were walking toward Kona.

"This is Vancouver and Victoria and Toronto," said Stumpy. "Not only do they know where we can find a truck stop, but they also know *exactly* where Kitten was when he was washed away from his mama."

The three geese nodded their heads vigorously, their long black necks giving them an air of authority.

"You can find a truck stop near the river on Marine Road," said Vancouver. The other two geese continued nodding their heads.

"That's one problem solved," said Stumpy.

"And," said Vancouver, "what that kitten saw was the Rest Area on Highway 65 up on the mountain."

"Plenty of big trucks there," said Victoria.

"And too much barking for me," said Toronto.

"Really?" asked Kona.

"Yes," said Toronto, "way too much barking."

"No, I mean, you're *really* sure? Kitten saw a Rest Area up on the mountain?" asked Kona.

"All the trucks stop there before they go down the other side of the mountain," said Victoria. "And it has a dog park too."

Stumpy looked at Kona. "The Rest Area has to be the place Kitten was trying to describe," she said.

"It's positively on our southern route," said Vancouver. "We know it well."

"Incredible!" said Kona.

"Oops, pardon me," said Toronto, suddenly turning his back to everyone.

CAH-AHNK!

"Sorry," he said, turning around again. "Fall cold." He wiped his nose with a wing.

"Oh dear," said Stumpy. She wished she'd brought tissues.

"What we need is help from the sky," said Kona to the three geese. "We need someone to spot the bobcat mama, then tell her to stay close to that Rest Area."

"Not me," said Toronto. "I have the sniffles."

"Oh, sniffle-shmiffle," said Victoria. "This is about a baby and his mama. We have to do it."

Toronto wiped his nose again.

"Okay," he said.

"When you find the mama," said Stumpy, "just tell her that her kitten will be at that Rest Area very soon. I'm sure that with three of you searching, you'll spot her."

"Oh, not three of us," said Victoria. "Forty-eight."

"Pardon?" said Stumpy.

"We're a team," said Victoria. "The whole flock goes. Alberta and Manitoba and Ontario and Quebec and—"

"Great!" said Kona. He was pretty sure he

didn't need to know forty-eight names, helpful as these Canada geese were.

"We'll go now," said Victoria.

"Now?" said Kona and Stumpy together.

And within what seemed merely seconds, the entire flock of Canada geese—all forty-eight of them, including the one with the sniffles—took off in a loud rush of honks and wings, forming a beautiful V as they pointed their long necks toward the mountain and the Rest Area on 65.

"I'm impressed," said Kona.

"Animals who migrate are really good at team-work," said Stumpy. "Like us!"

When Kona and Gwendolyn were alone later in the evening—Professor Albert sleeping bliss-fully beneath the flannel blanket he'd bought on sale that day—the two friends looked again at the highway map.

There it was: a symbol—according to the map

key—for a REST AREA right on top of Kit-ten's mountain!

"That has to be where his mama lost him," said Gwendolyn. "She was probably being so careful near those trucks."

"And near the

dogs, too," said Kona. Kona knew that dogs were not always nice. A cocker spaniel in the park had once nipped him on the ear just for walking by.

"How awful she must have felt," said Gwendolyn, "when instead of a truck or a dog, it was a gully that was the real danger, a gully that took her baby away."

"Yes," said Kona.

He thought about Top, Bottom, and Sparrow and how he would feel if a gully washed one of them away.

"All we need is for the geese to find her," said Kona, "and tell her Kitten is coming home."

"'Coming home,'" repeated Gwendolyn. "Such a lovely phrase, isn't it, dear?"

Kona nodded solemnly.

"Home is where someone loves you," said Gwendolyn. "No matter where it is. Or who the someone is."

"I guess the house on Paradise Lane was home for me," said Kona, "when I was still a puppy living with my mother. But I don't remember much. Professor Albert has always been my mother. If you know what I mean."

"I do," said Gwendolyn.

"And Morton," said Kona, "he didn't 'come home' until he found his brother, Murray, and Stumpy and the children living together in the park and he decided to stay."

"Yes," said Gwendolyn. "All the Zen meditation in the world cannot replace the warmth of someone who loves you."

Kona told Gwendolyn about Sparrow taking Kitten under her wing. About the string mittens. About the hugs and the kibble.

"Poor child," said Gwendolyn. "It will be hard for her to let him go."

Kona thought of Sparrow being unhappy, and he could hardly bear it.

"What can we do to help her?" he asked. "When Kitten goes away?"

"I think that when someone is sad," said

Gwendolyn, "it helps if a friend says simply, 'I'm sorry you are sad.'"

"I can say that," said Kona.

"You can ask Sparrow if she would like to talk about Kitten," continued Gwendolyn. "Especially the happy times they shared."

"That, too," said Kona.

"And perhaps remind her how much courage it takes to do what's best for someone you love," added Gwendolyn.

"It does," said Kona. "Maybe my mother felt all those things and had to have courage, too, to let her puppies live in different houses and be loved by someone else."

"I'm sure she did," said Gwendolyn.

"How many children did you say you have, Gwendolyn?" asked Kona.

"Oh, dozens, dear," she answered.

"That is a lot of good-byes," said Kona.

"It was time," said Gwendolyn. "There is always a time when good-bye is both a wonderful ending and a wonderful beginning. Life is like that. My children are having adventures all over the world because we knew when to say good-bye."

"That's so nice," said Kona.

"I do send them birthday cards telepathically every year, of course," Gwendolyn added.

"Of course," said Kona.

"And now let us firm up our plan for Kitten's return home," said Gwendolyn. "We have found a goose."

"Forty-eight of them," added Kona.

"Forty-eight geese," said Gwendolyn, "who have found the bobcat mama by now and have told her to wait at the Rest Area."

"We hope," said Kona.

"We have located a truck stop," continued Gwendolyn, "where you and Murray will take Kitten to find a truck going up the mountain."

"Yes," said Kona.

"Murray will find a truck with a friendly dog who doesn't mind sharing space with a bobcat and a bat. And Kitten will get a ride up the mountain to the Rest Area and find his mama," Gwendolyn concluded.

"Right," said Kona.

The two were silent a moment.

"If only Morton were here," said Kona, "he could give us an affirmation to repeat."

"Such as 'If you can dream it, you can do it'?" asked Gwendolyn.

"Exactly!" said Kona.

"Well, dear," said Gwendolyn, "if we can dream it . . ."

"We can do it!" said Kona.

And he actually felt that maybe they could.

8

Departure

Good-bye is hard when someone has grown fond of someone else, and this was as true in Gooseberry Park as anywhere.

The little bobcat kitten had grown very fond of Stumpy because she mothered him. And he had grown fond of the children because they sistered (Sparrow) and brothered him (Top and Bottom). He was fond of Murray because the bat was funny. And he was so fond of them all after only two days in the hollow log.

But Kitten was a baby, and he needed his mama. It was time for good-bye.

The next evening, the evening of departure, Kitten's friends prepared him for his trip home. Stumpy put some kibble in an old marbles bag to make sure he wouldn't be hungry, even though Murray had promised Kitten a slice of cheese pizza at the truck stop. All truck stops had pizza, Murray was pretty sure.

Top and Bottom wanted to give Kitten two of their little cars to take home, but Stumpy said they would weigh him down. So Top and Bottom gave Kitten stickers instead, which he stuck onto his tail.

"Thank you," said Kitten, admiring his tail.

And Sparrow. Sparrow didn't want Kitten to go home at all. She wanted to keep him. She wanted to hold on to her end of the string mittens forever. She did not want to say good-bye.

But Sparrow understood that Kitten needed his mama, just as she still needed hers. How sad for Kitten to be away from his mama. Even when he had such good friends who let him play with their cars and sniff their lavender sachets.

"Tell your mama hello for me," Sparrow told Kitten, combing down a stray piece of fur on his head.

"Okay," said Kitten.

He looked into Sparrow's eyes.

"Kitten hungry," he said.

Sparrow smiled.

"Do you mean 'sad'?" she asked.

"Sad," said Kitten.

"Me too," said Sparrow. She wrapped her arms around him and tried not to cry.

"Ta-da!" It was Murray coming in for a landing. "Reporting for duty!

"I was over at Kona's house," Murray said, "to check the map. Now, how did I not know about the Jubilee Truck Stop?"

He grinned at Kitten.

"We're going to love it," he said.

Kona arrived next, look-ing a bit frazzled but ready.

"I asked Gwendolyn to send some telepathic messages to Professor Albert to sleep in late," said Kona. "It could be almost sunrise before I get back home. I hope the geese have done their part."

"I'm sure they have," said Stumpy. "Canadians are so reliable.

"I just hope you can find a helpful dog quickly when you reach the truck stop," she added. "Everything depends on it."

"Don't worry," said Murray, "I've got that one figured out."

He pointed to a take-out bag he'd slyly dropped behind the tree.

"Moo shu pancakes," he said. "When a bat wants to make a friend."

"I think it's time to go," said Kona.

Sparrow hung the string mittens around Kitten's neck and patted his head.

"These will keep you close to your mama," she said.

Kitten purred.

Top and Bottom patted Kitten's head too.

"Will you write to us?" asked Bottom.

"Yes," said Kitten, even though he didn't know what "write" meant.

Stumpy helped Kitten up onto Kona's back. She hung the marbles sack of kibble and the Norm's bag of moo shu around Kona's neck.

"See you later, alligator," said Top.

The three children giggled. Even Sparrow.

Kitten smiled because they were smiling.

Then, before anyone could think of one more

 thing to say or one more bag to hang around Kona's neck, Kitten and Kona and Murray were off and away.

"*Good-bye!*" called the children. "*Good-bye!*"

Sparrow wiped away her tears. She understood. She held tight to her mama and wished for Kitten to find his.

9

The Jubilee

There is something about a long ride with an uncertain destination that puts many children right to sleep. Kitten was no exception.

Kona and Murray avoided the open roads and instead followed the path along the river that would lead to the Jubilee Truck Stop.

Kitten slept soundly on Kona's back,

bobcat claws digging into the dog's thick fur.

"Kitten has quite a grip," Kona commented as he walked steadily just ahead of Murray, who was doing loops in the air to amuse himself. Murray was used to traveling *fast*, and a four-legged dog was so slow that looping was the only way Murray could keep from pulling out his bat hair in frustration.

Kitten snored and purred and kneaded Kona's back. It had been a while since Kitten had had someone to snuggle against while he slept.

The moon was almost full this night, and it spread a glistening sheen over the water. Now and then a head popped up (from the river) or out (of a tree) as other creatures observed the looping bat and the dog with the bags and—*was that a cat on top of the dog?* But none of the creatures made a sound. Sometimes it is best just to let whatever is odd travel on.

It was a long walk, the longest walk Kona had ever taken.

"How do sled dogs run for fifty miles?" Kona said to Murray.

"On their feeties," answered the bat.

"I mean, how can they go so far? Wouldn't they get bored?" Kona asked. "Aren't you just a little bored?"

Murray flew upside down in front of Kona's nose.

"Nope," he said, looping right side up.

Kona sighed. What he missed, he realized, was the park. Gooseberry Park with all of its beautiful, familiar trees and paths and friends he knew by name. He missed Professor Albert's cheerful presence and the words "Good boy!"

Kona realized, walking along a new path to a new place, that he was actually, at heart, a homebody.

"Hey!" said Murray after several minutes. "Do you hear 'RRRR-RRRR-RRRR'?"

"I do," said Kona. "And I smell diesel."

"I smell dinner," said Murray.

And there it was: the Jubilee Truck Stop in all its magnificence. It was almost 4:00 a.m., and already twenty or so big rigs were preparing to roll. The sight was quite incredible. Kona and Murray marveled at the giant flashing JUBILEE sign on top of a tall pole, radiating over the land. There was a series of fuel pumps beside the truck stop, and a big rig was lined up at every one of them. More big rigs were parked in the parking lot—lit up like spacecraft—and their drivers were checking maps and clearing their cabs of old food boxes and old cups of coffee or putting in new food boxes and new cups of coffee. For the haul. These were the real thing: long-haul truckers.

Letters on the big front windows of the Jubilee advertised DELI WITH HOT MEALS, COFFEE AND DOUGHNUTS, PARK 'N' BARK DOG WASH.

"They even have a dog wash," said Murray.

"Amazing," Kona replied.

"I think we should live here," Murray said.

Just then Kitten woke up.

"Mama?" he asked.

"Not yet," said Murray. "But can you say 'cheesy fries'?"

The three travelers hid behind some oil drums to get a closer look.

Bark! Bark-bark! Bark-bark-bark!

It was too dark to see any of the dogs who were waiting inside the cabs of the trucks, but they could certainly hear them.

"Kona?" said Kitten, moving up closer against the dog's body.

"Don't worry, Kitten," said Kona. "You'll be safe. We'll wait here while Murray finds the right dog. Then *zip*, into a truck you'll go."

"With Murray?" asked Kitten.

"Absolutely," said Murray. "We are going to hide our little bodies in one of those rigs and go find your mama. Piece of cake."

"Cake?" asked Kitten.

"And probably pie," said Murray.

Kona smelled the diesel fuel and listened to the rumble of the loudest engines he'd ever heard and watched the truckers in boots and hats climb in and out of the giant cabs, and he hoped, more than ever, for a miracle. Or at least for a long-haul dog who liked moo shu.

10

C. A. T.

The nice thing about being a bat in the dark is that it's difficult to see a bat in the dark. And although much of the Jubilee Truck Stop was brightly lit, there were many dark hiding places where a sneaky little bat could watch what was going on.

But before he did anything important—like find *some transportation*—Murray did something *really* important: He snatched a slice of cheese pizza right off the front seat of a big rig and flew it back to Kitten.

"Told you!" said Murray. Then he flew off again.

It was just too easy. The truckers all had their windows rolled down while they were gassing up. They walked all around their rigs, proudly admiring the sparkling custom chrome grilles and aluminum rims, not having a clue that they were setting themselves up for a bat snatch.

Murray could have entertained himself for hours snatching pizza and fried shrimp baskets and who knows how many jelly doughnuts. But he didn't. He was *on duty*.

It didn't take Murray long, hanging around under the *B* in JUBILEE, to spot the right trucker and the right dog.

He saw a big rig in the parking lot with letters on the side of it that spelled "cat." C. A. T. *CAT!*

How crazy is that? thought Murray. *It's a CAT truck!*

Then he saw a trucker approaching the big rig. The trucker was wearing a hat with letters on it: C. A. T.

"I must be dreaming!" Murray said out loud. "That has to be our rig!"

The trucker was carrying a bag with something small and alive inside it.

Murray could see that the something was a tiny dog. Only bat vision could have seen a dog that small from the letter *B*.

Tiny dog equals extra room for Kitten and me! thought Murray. *Plus I'll get most of the food!*

He wished he could CB-radio all this new information to Kona.

The trucker put the dog inside the truck cab, then went back to the deli. It didn't take long for Murray to fly his sneaky bat self onto the top of the truck. Murray had completely forgotten to bring his moo shu pancakes, so all he had to work with was his charm. The window was open. He flew in.

"Ta-da!" he said. He did his little tappity-tap dance on the front seat.

"Ha-ha-ha-ha!"

It worked! Tiny Dog didn't seem to mind at all that a bat had flown in uninvited.

Yorkies (Tiny Dog was a Yorkie) are known to be quite agreeable when entertained, and Patsy (Patsy was the Yorkie's name) loved a show.

"Golly, you can dance!" said Patsy.

Murray was about to tell her all about the bob-cat kitten, when suddenly he spotted a big bag of jelly beans on the dashboard. He realized he was starving! He shoveled in a mouthful.

"Mob-bat mitten," he said to Patsy, gobbling as fast as he could, as drips of red, yellow, and green jelly-bean drool rolled down his chin.

"Pardon?" said Patsy.

Somehow, between mouthfuls, Murray was able to explain to Patsy why he—why he and a *cat* who happened to be a *bobcat*, but a little one— needed a ride up the mountain.

Patsy listened to the story and then said, "Well, you all come along! We've got plenty of room!"

Patsy was delighted to show Murray all the little cubbies behind the cab's sleeping curtain that were perfectly bat-and-kitten-sized, and where Jake—who was her owner and the best big-rig trucker ever—wouldn't see them while he drove up the mountain.

"We always stop at that Rest Area," said Patsy. "We see a lot of old friends there."

"If Kitten falls asleep," said Murray, "he'll probably snore. Can you howl or something to drown out the noise?"

"Oh, don't worry," said Patsy in her tiny Yorkie voice, "we listen to country all the way. It's *loud*. Jake has a woofer."

"COUNTRY?" repeated Murray. "I LOVE COUNTRY!"

So he flew back to get Kitten while Jake was stocking up on Twizzlers and other essentials for long-distance hauling.

Behind the oil drums, Kona put the marbles-bag of kibble around Kitten's neck, and he patted Kitten's head.

"Don't forget to write," said Kona.

"Okay," said Kitten.

Then, before anyone could blink twice, Murray flew and Kitten ran across the parking lot and jumped into the biggest and best transportation they could ever have imagined.

Jake showed up a few minutes later and cranked up the country, and away they went.

Kona watched the big rig roll away, and he had only one thought: *I'm exhausted.*

And he was hungry, too.

Then Kona remembered the moo shu pancakes that were still hanging around his neck.

He went back to the path beside the river and found a quiet place to sit and look at the water. Then Kona ate every bite of the pancakes Murray had forgotten, as he watched the tip of the sun begin to rise.

Renewed, Kona headed for home, running faster now, so he could make it back to Miller Street before Professor Albert's Mr. Coffee woke him up.

11

Together
Again

Every kid gets a souvenir!" said Murray, waving
the paper sack in the air.

It was the evening after Murray's ride up the
mountain with Kitten and Patsy and Jake, and
now all his friends had gathered in Professor
Albert's basement while the professor was away
at bingo. Life would soon be normal again. But
first the tale of rescuing a bobcat kitten needed to
come to a satisfying conclusion.

Murray reached into the sack and pulled out three key chains, with a different big rig on each one.

"Wow!" said Top, Bottom, and Sparrow.

"Mack for you, and Freightliner for you, and Western Star for you!" said Murray as he gave a key chain to each of Stumpy's children.

"Thank you!" said Top, Bottom, and Sparrow.

"I left the Jubilee Truck Stop so fast that I didn't get a chance to browse," said Murray. "So after I dropped Kitten off with his mama, I went back!

"Sorry I couldn't bring something for everybody," he added. "My feeties could hold only three presents and a doughnut."

"Oh, I have too many things anyway," said Stumpy.

"And I am a minimalist," said Gwendolyn.

"And I ate your moo shu," said Kona.

"How did you manage to snatch everything without getting caught?" asked Stumpy.

"You'd be surprised how a touchdown on a big-screen TV can get everyone's attention!" answered Murray.

"Anyway," he continued, "I used my fuzzy little bat wings to clean a couple of skylights, so I earned the loot!"

The children passed around their souvenir key chains as everyone felt the peacefulness that follows a happy outcome.

"If Jake had rolled up his windows when we got to the Rest Area, I guess Kitten and I would be in Texas by now," said Murray. "But Jake likes to leave them open a bit. So when he went with

Patsy to the dog park, Kitten and I squeezed our skinny little selves through the window! We were in the woods in a split second!"

"But how did you find the mama?" asked Sparrow.

"All Kitten had to do was meow," answered Murray, "and she was right there."

"Of course," said Gwendolyn. "She has a sixth sense."

"And good hearing," said Murray.

"Kitten would still be living in a hollow log in the park if not for the Canada geese," said Stumpy. "I wish we could thank them for finding Kitten's mama and telling her where to wait for him."

"I thought perhaps," said Gwendolyn, "I could put some of my natural cold remedy in a pouch for the flock to share. Kona could take it to them when they come back next spring."

"Toronto would love that," Stumpy said. "Winter is next for Gooseberry Park. I need to get back to foraging."

"Me too," said Murray. "Where would I be without Norm's?"

Kona looked around at all of his friends. How lucky he was. How lucky they all were, to be here and to have Kitten safe and sound with his mama.

Kona asked Murray if he could help bring

some refreshments down from the kitchen so that everyone would stay a little longer.

"Food? For this crowd?" said Murray. "No worries about the professor?"

"We can nibble on bits of this and that," said Kona, "so that he won't notice anything is missing."

"I love nibbling," said Murray.

"In return," said Kona, "I'll chew on some of the overgrown boxwoods tomorrow. Professor Albert likes them nicely clipped."

So Kona and Murray went up to the kitchen to fill up a plate with bits of this and that: bits of cheese, bits of raisins, bits of cranberries and blueberries and blackberries, bits of saltines and pecans and those miniature sugar cookies the children loved.

Kitten was home.

Everyone was together.

And all was well.